Bats at the Library

BY BRIAN LIES

HOUGHTON MIFFLIN COMPANY BOSTON

To Kate O'Sullivan, my first true
batvocate; to the librarians at the
Riverside (Ill.) Public Library, the
Duxbury (Mass.) Free Library, and
the Princeton (N.J.) Public Library;
and to Amy Tull, who told me
about that one winged
visitor without a library card...

ALPHABATS

www.houghtonmifflinbooks.com

The text of this book is set in 18-point Legacy.
The illustrations are acrylic paint on Strathmore paper.

Library of Congress Cataloging-in-Publication Data
Lies, Brian.
Bats at the library / written and illustrated by Brian Lies.
        p. cm.
Summary: Bored with another normal, inky evening, bats discover an open library window and fly in to enjoy
the photocopier, water fountain, and especially the books and stories found there.
ISBN 978-0-618-99923-1
[1. Stories in rhyme. 2. Bats—Fiction. 3. Libraries—Fiction. 4. Books and reading—Fiction.] I. Title.
PZ8.3.L5963Baq 2008
[E]—dc22
                              2008000597

Manufactured in China
WKT 10 9 8 7 6 5 4 3 2 1

Another inky evening's here—
the air is cool and calm and clear.
We've feasted, fluttered, swooped, and soared,
and yet . . . we're still a little bored.

All this *sameness* leaves us blue
and makes us ache for something new.
Then word spreads quickly from afar:
a window has been left ajar.

Can it be true? Oh, can it be?
Yes! — Bat Night at the library!

The sky is lively as we race
together toward our favorite place.
Eager wings beat autumn air—

Look, that's it. We're almost there!

Then squeezed together, wing to wing,
we rocket through the opening.

We've waited for this night all year,
but this is it! At last . . .

. . . we're here.

For most old bats, this isn't new—
they've got lots of things to do.
They'll flutter off and lose themselves
among the books lined up on shelves.

Other bats, in munchy moods,
will study guides to fancy foods
or hang out by a lamp instead
to talk about the books they've read.

But little bats will have to learn
the reason that we *must* return.
The ones who haven't come before
have no idea what's in store.

Some of them will drift away
and figure out a game to play,
like shaping shadows on the wall,
or wingtip-tag around the hall.

This big box is loads of fun,
blasting brighter than the sun.
Instead of copying books from shelves,
we can duplicate ourselves!

Doesn't matter where you look;
there's nothing like a pop-up book!

The fountain water's nice and cool
and makes a splendid swimming pool.

Please keep it down—you must *behave!*
This library is not your cave!

It's hard to settle down and read
when life flits by at dizzy speed.
But storytime is just the thing
to rest a play-exhausted wing.

And if we listen, we will hear
some distant voices drawing near—
louder, louder, louder still,
they coax and pull us in, until . . .

everyone—old bat or pup—
has been completely swallowed up
and *lives* inside a book instead
of simply hearing something read.

Breathless, lost within the tale,
no one sees the sky grow pale.

What is that light? A lamp? The moon?
Our bookish feast can't end so soon.

It feels as though we've just begun,
but now we leave our books half done.

Through the window, into sky—
it's much too late—we've got to fly.

But maybe a librarian
will give us bats this chance again—
and leave a window open wide
to let us share the world inside!

For now, we'll dream of things we've read,
a universe inside each head.
Every evening, one and all
will listen for that late-night call:

Can it be true? Oh, can it be?
Yes! — Bat Night at the library!